Indian Two Feet Rides Alone

By Margaret Friskey
Illustrated by John Hawkinson

 CHILDRENS PRESS, CHICAGO

Library of Congress Cataloging in Publication Data

Friskey, Margaret, 1901-
   Indian Two Feet rides alone.

  SUMMARY: A young Indian boy searches for a salt
lick so his people can have salt for their meat.
   [1. Indians of North America—Fiction]
I. Hawkinson, John, 1912-   II. Title.
PZ7.F918Ir   [E]   80-12688
ISBN 0-516-03523-1

Two Feet learned
something every day.
   He learned from the
woods.
   He learned from the
river.

3

He learned from the
hills and the animals.

He listened to the
talk around the fire.

"The good earth gives
us all we need," said
the old one.

"Grass feeds the deer
and buffalo. Clean water
flows from the hills.

"There are berries and
nuts for us to pick.

"The good earth gives us
clay for our pots. And
reeds for our baskets."

"The earth gives us salt
for our meat," said one
hunter.
"But we have no salt now,"
said another.

"I will find some salt," said Two Feet.

"Ask the deer where the salt lick lies," said the old one. "Ask the moose or the fox. Animals know where to find salt."

9

Two Feet rode off like
the wind.

"I am an Indian, Indian,
Indian!" he shouted. "Soon
I will know everything! I
will even know where the
salt lick lies."

The deer heard him and
fled into the woods.
The moose heard him and
swam across the river.

The fox heard him and
led her kits to the cave
in the hill.

13

Two Feet stopped to listen.

He heard birds flying away. He heard the river running by. He heard a rider coming.

An Indian girl, riding like the wind, caught up with him.

"I am going for salt," said Two Feet.

"Do you know where it is?"

"No. I will ask the deer or the moose or the fox," said Two Feet.

"You are as noisy as a herd of buffalo," said the girl. "An animal with any sense would flee. They all have fled."

"Oh," said Two Feet.

"But I know where the
salt is," said the girl.
"I was quiet as a shadow.
I followed the animals.
I will show you where
to go."
    They rode off together
to the salt lick.

Two Feet filled his bag.
"Why," thought Two Feet,
"she is just a girl. She can
ride as fast as I. But I will
show her what I alone can do."

He swam his horse
across the river.
    But she swam her horse
across the river, too.
    Then she waved to him
and rode away.

Two Feet could smell
meat cooking when he
reached the camp fire.
Proudly he held up his
bag of salt for all to see.

When the bag was opened,
the salt was soaking wet.

It had to be spread in the
sun to dry.

"Did the moose tell you
to dip it in the river?"
asked a hunter.

"I never met the moose,"
said Two Feet. "I made so
much noise all the animals
fled." He hung his head.

28

Two Feet looked up at the
old one. "But I met a girl,"
he said. "She quietly had
followed the animals. She
showed me where the salt
lick lay."

"Ah," said the old one.
"You have learned something
today!"
"From a GIRL?"
"From an INDIAN, my little
Two Feet," said the old one.

About the Author:

Margaret Friskey, Editor Emeritus of Childrens Press, was Editor-in-Chief of the company from its conception in 1945 until her retirement in 1971. It was under her editoral direction that Childrens Press expanded to become a major juvenile publishing house. Although she now has more free time, her days are by no means quiet. She spends time with her children and grandchildren, all of whom live near enough to her little house in Evanston to visit often. She also has more time to concentrate on her writing.

About the Artist:

An artist of wide-ranging interests, John Hawkinson recently wrote Childrens Press describing his current activities. "I am presently on a trip to New Zealand and Australia with my new wife, Peggy. We are birdwatching and lecturing school children. Peggy talks about the birds and I paint them. Last year we toured and lectured in England.

"When we aren't traveling we live in Winterhaven, Florida where my wife teaches ornithology and biology. I recently have been engaged by schools and other institutions to participate in their art grant programs. Because of my experience, I firmly believe that elementary schools should get back to the basics namely dance, music and art."